Young Authors' Day at Pokeweed Public School

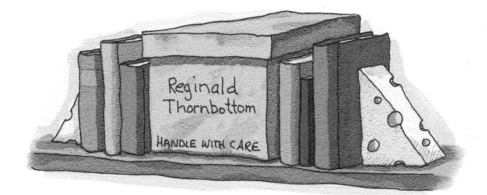

Written & Illustrated by

John Bianchi

Reading is so important at Pokeweed Public School that Ms. Mudwortz gives us some FRED each morning. FRED stands for Free Reading Every Day. When it's time for FRED, everyone finds a comfortable spot and settles down with a good book.

BOOK TUB

We all like different authors for different reasons.
Billy reads R.L. Mugs because his stories are so scary.

Buwocka always picks Tom Windysmith's books about sports.

Melody and I like the Mikki Merski Mysteries. We always try to see who can solve the mystery first.

But everyone loves Reginald Thornbottom's adventure
books. Ms. Mudwortz says that his stories are so exciting, they
are larger than life.

Each year, we devote a whole week to our school's young
authors. The week ends with a visit by a real author. And this
year — we could hardly believe it! — Reginald Thornbottom
was coming to Pokeweed Public School.

We started the week with Writing Day.

Ms. Mudwortz said that before we began our stories, we needed an idea. An idea could be about anything — like a toy or a game or a bird — something that interested us.

Then we had to have three things.

I have a plant. I call my plant Nancy. Nancy likes water. Nancy hates bugs.

First, we needed a beginning. Ms. Mudwortz called this part the "introduction."

"Write something about your idea," she told us.

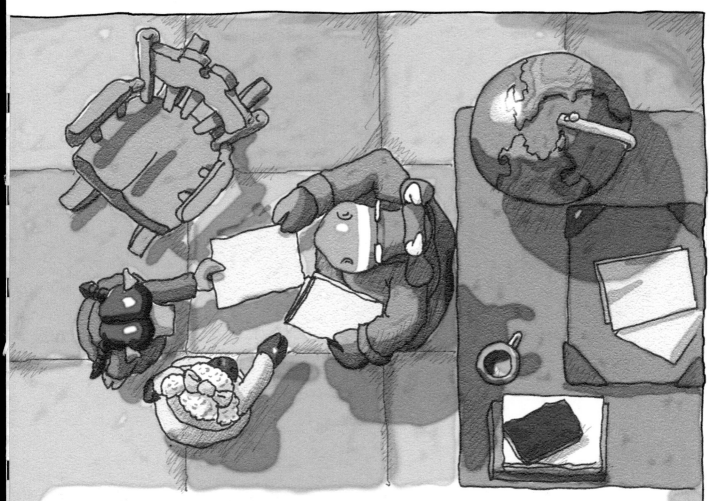

Tuesday was Picture Day, the day we "turned our words into pictures," as Ms. Mudwortz explained.

Then she gave us some tips:

"Make sure your character looks the same on each page."

"Try drawing your picture from very far away or very close up."

"Pretend you are a bird, looking down on your picture."

Wednesday was Book Day. We thought of a title for our story, we made a cover out of construction paper, and we bound our pages into real books.

On Thursday, FRED turned into RAT — Read Aloud Time. We each took turns reading our finished books to the class.

"A book is just a bunch of paper stuck together until someone reads it," said Ms. Mudwortz.

Then it was time to prepare for Reginald Thornbottom's visit. Since no one had ever seen a photograph of him, Ms. Mudwortz thought it would be fun for each of us to draw a picture of what we imagined he might look like. We couldn't wait to see who had come the closest.

Friday was Young Authors' Day.

Ms. Mudwortz assembled the band outside, and when we saw Reginald Thornbottom's car pull up, we all played *For He's a Jolly Good Fellow*.

"Welcome to Pokeweed Public School, Mr. Thornbottom," said Principal Slugmeyer, rushing him into the school.

"But . . . ," he replied.

"Time for a fast photo," ordered Principal Slugmeyer, as he arranged everyone in the library.
"But . . . ," said our guest, as the camera flashed.

Principal Slugmeyer hurried him to the auditorium and up onto the stage.

"Everyone's in place," said Principal Slugmeyer, looking out at the crowd.

"But . . . ," whispered our visitor.

As Ms. Mudwortz raised her hoof to silence everyone, Principal Slugmeyer made an enthusiastic introduction.

"Okay, everyone, let's put our paws and hooves together and give a warm Pokeweed Public School welcome to Mr. Reginald Thornbottom!"

"Thank you very much," our guest of honor began after an enormous ovation. "I'm pleased to be here. But I'm not Reginald Thornbottom!"

We all gasped.

"I'm Arthur, Mr. Thornbottom's driver."

"But . . . but what happened to Mr. Thornbottom?" asked Principal Slugmeyer. "Is he ill? Did he have an accident? Did he get lost?"

"Oh, no. He's right here," announced Arthur, opening the box he was carrying.

"Hello," squeaked Reginald Thornbottom as Arthur lifted him out.

"I . . . I thought that was a box of books," said Principal Slugmeyer, shaking the tiny author's paw.

"Of course not," corrected Mr. Thornbottom. "It's my office. Arthur takes me everywhere in it. The world is a dangerous place for a little book mouse like me. And besides, I never like to be far from my work — so I bring it with me!"

And with that, little Reginald Thornbottom proceeded to give a great big presentation.

First, he showed us some pictures of where he lives and where he does his work and some of the neat places he has been.

Then he demonstrated some of his writing techniques.

He talked about how he always uses big sheets of paper so that he has lots of room to expand his ideas.

Finally, he read to us from his latest book. When his presentation was finished, we ended the afternoon with the annual Young Authors' Pizza Party.

Young Authors' Day was another classic Pokeweed Public School success. Mr. Thornbottom even took the time to read and autograph all our books.

I love what he put in mine. "Keep up the good work!" he wrote. "And remember, you don't have to be big to write stories that are larger than life."